This book belongs to:

_____

by
Joyce Cuchelo

little pink press

Illustrations by April Matula

Published by Little Pink Press, P.O. Box 847, Beacon, NY 12508

ISBN-13: 978-1-7355918-1-0

Miss Martha Menk was very fat
and very ugly too!

She couldn't help the way she looked...

It's just the way she GREW.

Everywhere Miss Martha went,
people stopped and stared.

Small children screamed and ran away,

and no one even cared.

The older boys and girls would laugh,
and then, to her they'd say,

"UGLY WITCH, JUST GO AWAY.
GO SOMEWHERE ELSE TO STAY!"

And then Miss Martha sat and cried,
at times, all day and night.

"Nobody wants to talk to me,
nor visit, it's not right!"

One day, Miss Martha heard a noise
while she was sitting home.

She found a little, baby cat,
crying and all alone...

The cat was hungry, tired, and cold.

Miss Martha picked him up.

And brought him to her little house.

Then fed him from a cup.

Now Boo, the cat was happy there.
He'd jump, and run, and play...

And when he'd purr and rub her leg,
SHE KNEW THAT HE WOULD STAY!

Quite soon the other cats and dogs
came by to visit too.

Miss Martha fed them LOTS of food
and watched them play with Boo.

The children watched their little pets
go wandering away...

They followed all the cats and dogs
to see where they would play.

The children tiptoed down the road.
They followed all the way,
right to Miss Martha's little house...

What would their parents say???

The children stood there for a time.
They didn't run away!

Miss Martha wasn't ugly...fat...
"Wow, she's so kind! Let's stay."

A party we are going to have.
There's food for everyone.
A cake and ice cream...popcorn too.
Please stay...oh, please don't run.

"We'll have to ask our mom and dad
if we may visit you."

Miss Martha smiled, and then she said,
"Please come and bring them, too!"

The party was such super fun,
for there was lots to do.

They ate and laughed and played some games.
Miss Martha played them too!

Now, every day, right after school,
everyone hurries...where?

A special place where love is found,
Miss Martha will be there!

Remember:

If someone doesn't look the way you think
they should, get to know them first.
They may be kind and good.

But, never go with a stranger,
(a person you don't know).
And, always tell your parents
where you plan to go!

Made in the USA
Middletown, DE
05 April 2021